JULIE
and the
duckling

Illustrations by José-Luis Macias S.
Original story by J. Barnabé Dauvister
Retold by Jane Carruth

Oh! Look Muffin, a little duckling has got his feet caught in some ivy leaves. Let's go and help him quickly!

Under Muffin's watchful eye, Julie saves the baby duck. He was really trapped. What would he have done without Julie and Muffin? He might have died.

"A nice warm bath will make you feel much better," says Julie! Petranella seems to smile as she watches her little mistress bathing the duckling, while Muffin gets the towel ready.

All the friends meet in the playroom. The little duck must be properly dried. He must not catch cold.

"He's lucky," sighs Muffin, as Julie comforts her new friend.

What a joke! Julie has put Petranella's hat on Yellow Beak's head – that's the name she has given to the pretty little duckling.

One little girl sitting on a swing,
tra-la! Everyone is having fun!
Muffin chats to a snail and
Yellow Beak chases after a
butterfly.

Now it's Julie's turn to put on a pretty hat. "This is my cooking hat, everyone. I'm going to make a lovely meal for you!"

Yellow Beak has eaten too much. Now he's ready for his sleep. Julie strokes him gently. She hopes he will have lovely dreams.

Next day Julie wants to wash, but
Yellow Beak is having a nice swim
in her bath!

Quick, it's time to go to school!

Julie has taken her satchel. Muffin runs along beside her. "I'm so excited about showing Yellow Beak to my friends. What fun we're all going to have playing together . . ." she tells him.

Susan, Nicola and Sarah
admire Yellow Beak.
They think he is sweet.

"Be careful!
He'll bite your finger!" warns Julie.

The teacher is extremely
cross. Little ducks are not
allowed in school. Julie is
so upset she does not know
what to do.

Her eyes are full of tears. How can she leave
Yellow Beak alone when she is at school?

"Hey, Muffin, you look after him. You can both go for a run on
the grass. Teacher is right, school isn't meant for ducklings!"

When she comes out of school, Julie says goodbye to the
duckling. He has found his mummy again. "We'll stay
friends!" shouts Julie. And Muffin barks, "I'll be your friend
too!"

Published in the United States and simultaneously in Canada by Joshua Morris, Inc.
431 Post Road East, Westport, CT 06880
Printed in Belgium